W9-BXV-505

GRAYSON COUNTY LIBRARY
INDEPENDENCE, VA 24348

HERE COMES THE CAT! / СЮДА ИДЕТ КОТ!

FRANK ASCH VLADIMIR VAGIN

SCHOLASTIC INC. NEW YORK

JE
Asc

Copyright © 1989 by Frank Asch and Vladimir Vagin.
All rights reserved. Published by Scholastic Inc.
SCHOLASTIC HARDCOVER is a registered trademark
of Scholastic Inc.

No part of this publication may be reproduced in whole or in part, or stored in a retrieval system, or transmitted in any form or by any means, electronic, mechanical, photocopying, recording, or otherwise, without written permission of the publisher. For information regarding permission, write to Scholastic Inc., 730 Broadway, New York, NY 10003.

Library of Congress Cataloging-in-Publication Data
Asch, Frank.
Here comes the cat!
Summary: Cat's arrival causes excitement among residents
of a mouse settlement. Text is in both English
and Russian.
[1. Friendship — Fiction. 2. Cats — Fiction.
3. Mice — Fiction. 4. Russian language materials — Bilingual]
I. Vagin, Vladimir Vasilévich, 1937–. II. Title.
PZ63.A725 1989 [E] 88-3083
ISBN 0-590-41859-9

12 11 10 9 8 7 6 5 4 3 2 1 9/8 0 1 2 3 4/9
Printed in the U.S.A. 36
First Scholastic printing, March 1989

In Russian,

СЮДА ИДЕТ КОТ!

means *Here Comes the Cat!*

and is pronounced

syu-DAH ee-DYOT KOT!

To my son,

DEVIN

—FRANK ASCH

To my daughter,

NASTIYA

—VLADIMIR VAGIN

35943

HERE COMES THE CAT!
СЮДА ИДЕТ КОТ!
quakk!
КРЯ!

GOOD DAY!
ДОБРЫЙ ДЕНЬ!
HELLO!
ПРИВЕТ!

СЮДА ИДЕТ КОТ!
HERE COMES THE CAT!

HERE COMES THE CAT!
СЮДА ИДЕТ КОТ!

HERE COMES THE CAT!
СЮДА ИДЕТ КОТ!
BOOM! БУМ!

BOOM!
БУМ!

HERE COMES THE CAT!
СЮДА ИДЕТ КОТ!

OUCH!
ОЙ!

СЮДА ИДЕТ КОТ!
HERE COMES THE CAT!

HERE COMES THE CAT!
СЮДА ИДЕТ КОТ!

BANK
БАНК
HERE COMES THE CAT!
СЮДА ИДЕТ КОТ!
SHOE STORE
ОБУВЬ

Tailor
Портной
CINIMA
КИНО
NOW
STARIVA:
В ФИЛЬМЕ
УЧАСТВУЮТ:
ICE CREAM
МОРОЖЕНОЕ
MICE AT WORK
МЫШКА НА РАБОТЕ

TOY STORE
ИГРУШКИ
СЮДА ИДЕТ КОТ!
HERE COMES THE CAT!
СЮДА ИДЕТ КОТ!
HERE COMES THE CAT!
HERE COMES THE CAT!
СЮДА ИДЕТ КОТ!

HERE COMES THE CAT!
СЮДА ИДЕТ КОТ!
СЮДА ИДЕТ КОТ!
HERE COMES THE CAT!
HERE COMES THE CAT!
СЮДА ИДЕТ КОТ!
HERE COMES THE CAT
СЮДА ИДЕТ КОТ!
HERE COMES THE CAT!
СЮДА ИДЕТ КОТ!

EXIT
ВЫХОД
СЮДА ИДЕТ КОТ!
HERE COMES THE CAT!

HOSPITAL
БОЛЬНИЦА
HERE COMES THE CAT!
СЮДА ИДЕТ КОТ!
СЮДА ИДЕТ КОТ!
HERE COMES THE CAT!
СЮДА ИДЕТ КОТ!
HERE COMES THE CAT!
СЮДА ИДЕТ КОТ!
HERE COMES THE CAT!
СЮДА ИДЕТ КОТ!
HERE COMES THE CAT!
СЮДА ИДЕТ КОТ!
HERE COMES THE CAT!
HERE COMES THE CAT!
СЮДА ИДЕТ КОТ!
HERE COMES THE CAT!
HERE COMES THE CAT!

HERE COMES THE CAT!
СЮДА ИДЕТ КОТ!
СЮДА ИДЕТ КОТ!
HERE COMES THE CAT!

MICE AT WORK
МЕЦИ НА РАБОТЕ
MMM-GOOD!
MMM-ВКУСНО!

MILK
МОЛОКО

WYTHE-GRAYSON REGIONAL LIBRARY
1000035943
99

35943

JE
Asc Asch, Frank

Here comes the cat.

Grayson County Public Library

Independence, Virginia 24348
(703) 773-2761

GRAYSON COUNTY LIBRARY
INDEPENDENCE, VA 24348